SANJU SAMSON

INDIAN CRICKETER

MR VIVEK KUMAR PANDEY

Short Biography Of Sanju Samson & Life Style, Career etc. During Writing This Book No Character, No Religion & No Caste Are Harmed. It's Only For Study Purpose.

Contents

Foreword

Author biography in English :

MY NAME IS VIVEK KUMAR PANDEY . I WAS BORN IN 30 SEP 2002,I AM FROM SURAT GUJARAT INDIA.MY DREAM WAS TO BE GOOD WRITERS ,MY FAMILY SUPPORTED ME TO SUCCESSFUL AND I CAN DO IT MY SELF.How do I write? That is a question, I believe, that can be honestly answered by me."CELEBRATING YOUNGEST WRITER AWARD WINNER IN GUJARAT 1ST RANK" MR PANDEY JI . I may think I did a good job writing something. The reader is the one who decides the quality of my writing. I do find writing to be natural to me and therefore find it to be a real challenge. My trick as a challenged writer is to do the best I can and know that I am happy with the final outcome. It may take a while to do my best and there may be quite a few problems I run into along the way.

I am not a greedy person those who are thinking about me and my self I never tried it anyone people suffering from sadness ,I trying to get promoted people suffering from happiness and joy in your Life Time. Now in current situation in India and also world people are unemployed and have no many but our indian governor help to people to get free food from ration card , i also take part in leadership team ,i am Motivational speakcr , Fllm script writer. There was my two dream firstly writer and secondly actor & also my own film is upcoming soon i done almost completely completed script for my film .I AM GOING TO SAY WORD OF HEART TOUCH OUT PLEASE READ IT" , firstly i thanks my father he supports me in this field they always getting inspired me by own his words and behavior ,they always said that he was a biggest person in the world in future and also they purchase fruit and chocolate for me in anytime & anyway , firstly my father buy him then call me Vivek you want a chocolate i will say yes papa but how many tell me ,papa: you tell me how much i buy him i told 1 or 2 chocolate but my father purchase whole the boxes of chocolate and they get suprised me. MY FATHER WAS BORN IN " 20 SEPTEMBER" 1971 IN INDIA.

1) MY FATHER FAVORITE CLOTHES IS KURTA PAIJMA AND ALSO STYLES SHOE

2) FAVORITE SINGER IS KISHORE DA

3) FAVORITE STATE GUJARAT AND KOLKATA , HIS VILLAGE IN BIHAR

4) FAVORITE COLOR BLACK AND WHITE

THEY ALSO LOVE cricket like IPL and one day t-20 .they also like watching a News daily and heard the song daily ,they also interested in tik tok video but in current time tik tok is banned in india but also few videos are in you tube. In lockdown time my family and me very enjoy day daily. my father play daily ludo with his sister and son, daughter.they always loved tea and coffee anytime call me ". I make it tea for my father but some reason after the April to june they are suffering from fever and cough , weakness on 6 June 2020 my father death. they not told me say bye bye his life. After death of 6 June on 10 june my mom and dad anniversary.but my father is Best in the world they can do anything for me please take care of father and respect it of your parents.

CHAPTER ONE

Sanju Samson

- *Sanju Samson*

Sanju Viswanath Samson (born 11 November 1994) is an Indian international cricketer who captains Kerala in domestic cricket and Rajasthan Royals in Indian Premier League. A right-handed top-order batter and wicketkeeper, he was the vice-captain of the Indian U-19 team for the 2014 Under-19 Cricket World Cup. He made his India debut in the 2015 away T20I against Zimbabwe. He made his ODI debut in 2021 against Sri Lanka.

Sanju started his cricketing career in Delhi and later moved to Kerala in his early teens. After creating waves in junior cricket, he made his first-class debut for Kerala in 2011. He made his IPL debut in 2013 for Rajasthan Royals and won the Emerging Player of the Year. He scored an unbeaten 212 in the 2019-20 Vijay Hazare Trophy in the sixth instance an Indian scored a double-century in List A cricket, which is also the second-fastest double ton in the format.

Sanju was born on 11 November 1994 into a Latin Catholic Malayali family in Pulluvila, a coastal village near Vizhinjam in Thiruvananthapuram district of Kerala.His father, Samson Viswanath, was formerly a police constable at Delhi Police and a retired football player who has represented Delhi in Santhosh Trophy and his mother, Ligy Viswanath is a housewife. His elder brother Saly Samson has represented Kerala in Junior cricket and currently works in the AG's office.

Sanju spent his early childhood in the Police residential colony in North Delhi neighbourhood of GTB Nagar and studied at Rosary Senior Secondary School, Delhi. He trained under coach Yashpal at the academy in DL DAV Model School, Shalimar Bagh. When Sanju didn't make it into the Delhi U-13 team for Dhruv Pandove Trophy, his father took voluntary retirement from the Delhi police force; a year after he retired from football and moved to Kerala, where Sanju and his brother continued their cricketing careers. In Kerala, he attended Masters Cricket Club in Thiruvananthapuram before changing academies to train under Biju George on Medical College Ground, Thiruvananthapuram.

Sanju graduated high school from St. Joseph's Higher Secondary School, Thiruvananthapuram, Kerala. He pursued a B.A. degree in English literature from Mar Ivanios College, Thiruvananthapuram. Apart from cricket, his childhood aspiration was to become an IPS officer.

- Youth career

Sanju was a member of the U-13 cricket team of Kerala in 2007. In the KSCA Inter-State under-13 tournament, he captained Kerala and bagged the player of the tournament award scoring 973 runs, including four centuries in five matches at an average of 108.11.As a member of Kerala U-15 team for the 2008-09 Vijay Merchant Trophy, he scored a double century off 138 balls against Goa and finished the tournament as the second-highest run-scorer with 498 runs including two centuries and two fifties.He was also the captain of Kerala in U-16 and U-19 levels.

His performance in the 2010-11 Cooch Behar Trophy earned him a spot in the India U-19 team that played the 2012 ACC Under-19 Asia Cup held in Malaysia in June 2012. His dismal show in the tournament meant that he failed to get selected to India's squad for the 2012 Under-19 Cricket World Cup that followed. He was named vice-captain of India U-19 team for the 2013 Top End Under-19 Series in Australia in June 2013. He scored two half-centuries in India U-19's Youth Test series against Sri Lanka held from July to August 2013. In the 2013 ACC Under 19 Asia cup in UAE, he scored a century in the final against Pakistan, helping India retain the cup. He was also India's vice-captain in the tournament. In January 2014, BCCI appointed Sanju as vice-captain of team India for the 2014 Under-19 Cricket World Cup. He was the top run-scorer for India in the tournament with a highest score of 85 runs from 45 balls against Papua New Guinea.

- domestic career

A double-century in the 2008-09 Vijay Merchant Trophy paved way to the Kerala squad for the 2009-10 Ranji Trophy.Then aged 14, he was the youngest Kerala cricketer to be selected to play in Ranji Trophy. He was named in the Kerala squad for the 2009-10 Syed Mushtaq Ali Trophy the same year. He made his first-class debut for the side in the 2011-12 Ranji Trophy on 3 November 2011 against Vidarbha and Twenty20 debut on 16 October 2011 against Hyderabad in the 2011-12 Syed Mushtaq Ali

Trophy. He was named in the Kerala squad for playing the 2011-12 Vijay Hazare Trophy and made his List-A debut on 23 February 2012 against Andhra Pradesh in the season.

He scored moderately in the 2012–13 Vijay Hazare Trophy in which Kerala featured in the semi-finals. He scored his maiden first-class century against Himachal Pradesh in the 2012-13 Ranji Trophy, as he scored 127 runs off 207 balls. He was Kerala's highest run-getter in 2013-14 Ranji Trophy season scoring 530 runs at an average of 58.88.In his first match of the 2013-14 season against Assam he scored a career-best 211 to bring up his first double century in Ranji Trophy. In the second match against Andhra Pradesh he scored 115 from 281 balls in the 1st innings followed by 51* in the second innings.He was named in South Zone's squad to play in the 2013-14 Deodhar Trophy in March 2014.On the Australia A Team Quadrangular Series in 2014, he finished as India A's highest run-scorer with 244 runs from seven innings, with an average of 81.33. He scored his second first-class double century in the 2014-15 Ranji Trophy.He was named in South Zone's squad to play in the 2014-15 Deodhar Trophy in November 2014.

- Inconsistent seasons

Sanju was appointed as the captain of Kerala for the 2015–16 Ranji Trophy season. Then aged 20, he is the youngest Kerala player to captain the state in Ranji Trophy. He began the season with a ton[but failed to convert it into a successful season.

He started the next Ranji season scoring a 154 against Jammu and Kashmir but again failed to impress the rest of the season. He was issued a show-cause notice by Kerala

Cricket Association for alleged acts of indiscipline during a match in the tournament.

- Sanju Return to form

Sanju was the leading run-scorer for Kerala in the 2017–18 Ranji Trophy, with 627 runs from seven matches. In a must-win match against Saurashtra, he scored a 68 in the first innings and smashed a 180 ball 175 in the second innings, helping his team claim a 309 runs victory and quarter-final berth. Kerala went on to play its first quarter-final in Ranji Trophy history in the season with Samson being one of their top performers.

In November 2017, he was appointed as the captain of the Board President's XI, replacing an injured Naman Ojha for a two-day tour match against Sri Lanka. He scored a century against the visiting team ending the match in a draw.

In August 2018, he was one of eight players that were fined by the Kerala Cricket Association, after showing dissent against Kerala's captain, Sachin Baby.

In September 2019, he scored 91 runs off 48 balls in the fifth unofficial List-A match between India A and South Africa A team and was awarded the man-of-the-match award.In October 2019, during the 2019–20 Vijay Hazare Trophy match between Kerala and Goa, Sanju doubled his maiden List-A century.] It was the second-fastest double hundred and the fastest by an Indian in the format. It was also the highest total made by a wicket-keeper in a List-A match with an unbeaten 212 runs from 129 balls. His partnership of 338 runs with Kerala skipper Sachin Baby in the match is the highest in List-A cricket for Indian cricket and the third highest in the format. The impact made from this innings went on to earn him a national call-up after four years, as he was selected to play the Bangladesh series that followed.

He was named the captain of Kerala ahead of the 2020–21 Syed Mushtaq Ali Trophy. Kerala played the quarter-finals of the 2021-22 Syed Mushtaq Ali Trophy and 2021-22 Vijay Hazare Trophy under his leadership.

- International cricket

In August 2014, Sanju was selected to India's 17-man squad to play in 5 ODIs and a Twenty20 against England. However, he did not make it to the final eleven in any of the matches and remained a backup keeper to MS Dhoni. In October 2014, he was called to the Twenty20 team to play a solitary T-20 against West Indies, which later got cancelled. In December 2014, he was named in India's 30-member probables list for the 2015 Cricket World Cup. In July 2015, he was drafted into the Indian squad against Zimbabwe for an ODI and two T20I matches as an injury replacement for Ambati Rayudu. He made his T20I debut against Zimbabwe at Harare on 19 July 2015. After a top-order collapse, Samson added 36 runs in the sixth wicket, along with Stuart Binny in a low-score chase. India eventually lost the match to Zimbabwe by 10 runs.

In October 2019, he was recalled to the Indian side after four years as a part of India's Twenty20 International (T20I) squad for their series against Bangladesh but was benched in the whole series.In November 2019, he was added to the Indian team for T20I series against West Indies after an injury to Shikhar Dhawan. In December 2019, he was named in the Twenty 20 squad to play against Sri Lanka. He featured in the third T20I and was dismissed in the second ball, after hitting the first for a sixer. He was selected for the T20I series of the India tour of New Zealand replacing an injured Shikhar Dhawan but failed to create the desired impact with the bat with a string of low scores.

"Sanju was fearless at the top of the order. He tried to take the momentum away, he should back himself".

Virat Kohli on Samson's batting on Team India.

In October 2020, he was named in India's Twenty20 International (T20I) squad for their series against Australia. On 9 November 2020, he was added to India's One Day International (ODI) squad, also for their series against Australia. He played all the three Twenty20s but flattered to deceive. He was dropped from India's Twenty20 International squad for their next series against England.

In June 2021, he was named in India's One Day International (ODI) and Twenty20 International (T20I) squads for their series against Sri Lanka.He made his ODI debut on 23 July 2021, for India against Sri Lanka. He disappointed with the bat in the T20 series in which a depleted Team India lost to Sri Lanka. He missed out from the Indian squad for the 2021 ICC Men's T20 World Cup, held in October 2021.

In February 2022, he was named in India's T20 squad for their series against Sri Lanka. He didn't bat in the first innings but scored 39 and 18 in the next two matches.In June 2022, he was named in India's squad for their T20I series against against Ireland. In the second match of the series, he scored his maiden half century in T20I, making 77 runs off 42 balls. His partnership with Deepak Hooda of 176 runs was the highest partnership for the second wicket in men's T20I and the highest partnership for any wicket for India.

In June 2022, he was named in India's squad for the first T20I of their series against England, but didn't feature in the starting eleven. In July 2022, he was named in India's ODI squad for their away series against the West Indies. He scored his maiden ODI half-century in the second match of the series. His 99-run partnership with Shreyas Iyer in the fourth wicket set the foundation for India's victory. On 29 July 2022, he was added to India's Twenty 20 International (T20I) squad, also for their series against West Indies, after KL Rahul tested positive for COVID-19. The same month, he was named in India's One Day International (ODI) squad for their series against Zimbabwe. In the second ODI against Zimbabwe, he scored an unbeaten 43 and took three catches and was declared the man of the match.

Sanju was named by Kolkata Knight Riders in its player pool ahead of 2009 Indian Premier League. He was signed by Kolkata Knight Riders ahead of 2012 Indian Premier League but did not get to play and was released ahead of the 2013 season. He was signed to play for Rajasthan Royals in 2013. He made his IPL debut for Rajasthan against Kings XI Punjab on 14 April 2013 after the regular wicket-keeper Dishant Yagnik failed to recover from an injury. In his second match, he scored 63 runs from 41 balls, becoming the then youngest player in IPL to score a half-century. He won the Best Young Player award of 2013 season with 206 runs and six stumpings from 10 innings.

Sanju made his Champions League Twenty20 debut for Rajasthan Royals against the Mumbai Indians on 21 September 2013 and scored 54 off 47 balls, becoming the youngest player to score a half-century in CLT20. He was retained by Rajasthan ahead of the 2014 season.

In 2016, Delhi Daredevils signed Sanju after Rajasthan was banned from the competition for two years after being found guilty in illegal betting and match-fixing probe. He scored his maiden T20 century against Rising Pune Supergiants during the 2017 Indian Premier League.

He returned to Rajasthan in the 2018 IPL auction He scored his second IPL century in the next season, hitting an unbeaten 102* against Sunrisers Hyderabad. During the 2020 season, Sanju scored a 32-ball 74 against Chennai Super Kings. He led Rajasthan to the highest successful run chase in IPL history with 85 runs from 42 balls against Kings XI Punjab in the next match. He played his 100th IPL match, later in the season.

- "You're a captain when you're fielding, not when you're batting".

In January 2021, Sanju was named the captain of Rajasthan Royals ahead of the 2021 Indian Premier League. He scored a century in his first match as captain, becoming the first IPL captain to achieve the feat. He completed 3000 runs in IPL later in the season.

In November 2021, he was retained by Rajasthan Royals ahead of the 2022 Indian Premier League. Sanju surpassed Ajinkya Rahane to become the all-time leading run-scorer for Rajasthan during the season. Rajasthan went on to play the finals and finished as the runners-up under his leadership.

- Playing style

Sanju is a naturally aggressive and elegant batsman who is hailed as a natural talent with quality batting techniques and wicket-keeping skills. He is considered an excellent timer of the ball who mostly sticks to his range between cover and fine-leg.He has the ability to play straight and prefers to hit straight over the bowler's head. Equipped with fast hands, powerful forearms and excellent hand-eye coordination, he prefers to stay still at the crease and rarely moves down the track to play shots. He can play aerial shots without moving his head.

His power has been compared to powerful stroke-makers such as Rohit Sharma and AB de Villiers who can middle the ball to play shots with seemingly minimal effort. His batting style has been described as "fearless" in Twenty20 cricket.

He is also an athletic fielder who generally fields in the outfield, but is flexible to field in any position. He has been often criticized for being inconsistent over the years. He has also been often criticized for his shot selections and temperament.

As of 2016, Sanju is working as the manager of Bharat Petroleum, Thiruvananthapuram. In 2018, he started a sports academy, namely "Six Guns Sports Academy", devoted to cricket and football training for young players in Thiruvananthapuram.He was appointed as the State election icon of Kerala, ahead of the 2021 Kerala Legislative Assembly election.

• Sanju Personal life

Sanju announced his marriage with his long-time girlfriend Charulatha Remesh, a native of Thiruvananthapuram, on 8 September 2018 through his social media platforms. The couple were college-mates from Mar Ivanios College. The marriage took place in a private ceremony at Kovalam on 22 December 2018. The wedding reception took place in Nalanchira on the same day with the only notable cricketer to attend being Sanju's former coach and mentor, Rahul Dravid.

CHAPTER TWO

What Is Cricket ?

- What Is Cricket ?

Cricket is a bat-and-ball game played between two teams of eleven players on a field at the centre of which is a 22-yard (20-metre) pitch with a wicket at each end, each comprising two bails balanced on three stumps. The game proceeds when a player on the fielding team, called the bowler, "bowls" (propels) the ball from one end of the pitch towards the wicket at the other end. The batting side's players score runs by striking the bowled ball with a bat and running between the wickets, while the bowling side tries to prevent this by keeping the ball within the field and getting it to either wicket, and dismiss each batter (so they are "out"). Means of dismissal include being bowled, when the ball hits the stumps and dislodges the bails, and by the fielding side either catching a hit ball before it touches the ground, or hitting a wicket with the ball before a batter can cross the crease line in front of the wicket to complete a run. When ten batters have been dismissed, the innings ends and the teams swap roles. The game is adjudicated by two umpires, aided by a third umpire and match referee in international matches.

Forms of cricket range from Twenty20, with each team batting for a single innings of 20 overs and the game generally lasting three hours, to Test matches played over five days. Traditionally cricketers play in all-white kit, but in limited overs cricket they wear club or team colours. In addition to the basic kit, some players wear protective gear to prevent injury caused by the ball, which is a hard, solid spheroid made of compressed leather with a slightly raised sewn seam enclosing a cork core layered with tightly wound string.

The earliest reference to cricket is in South East England in the mid-16th century. It spread globally with the expansion of the British Empire, with the first international matches in the second half of the 19th century. The game's governing body is the International Cricket Council (ICC), which has over 100 members, twelve of which are full members who play Test matches. The game's rules, the Laws of Cricket, are maintained by Marylebone Cricket Club (MCC) in London. The sport is followed primarily in South Asia, Australasia, the United Kingdom, southern Africa and the West Indies.Women's cricket, which is organised and played separately, has also achieved international standard. The most successful side playing international cricket is Australia, which has won seven One Day International trophies, including five World Cups, more than any other country and has been the top-rated Test side more than any other country.

- History of cricket to 1725

A medieval "club ball" game involving an underhand bowl towards a batter. Ball catchers are shown positioning themselves to catch a ball. Detail from the Canticles of Holy

Mary, 13th century.

Cricket is one of many games in the "club ball" sphere that basically involve hitting a ball with a hand-held implement; others include baseball (which shares many similarities with cricket, both belonging in the more specific bat-and-ball games category), golf, hockey, tennis, squash, badminton and table tennis. In cricket's case, a key difference is the existence of a solid target structure, the wicket (originally, it is thought, a "wicket gate" through which sheep were herded), that the batter must defend. The cricket historian Harry Altham identified three "groups" of "club ball" games: the "hockey group", in which the ball is driven to and fro between two targets (the goals); the "golf group", in which the ball is driven towards an undefended target (the hole); and the "cricket group", in which "the ball is aimed at a mark (the wicket) and driven away from it".

It is generally believed that cricket originated as a children's game in the south-eastern counties of England, sometime during the medieval period.Although there are claims for prior dates, the earliest definite reference to cricket being played comes from evidence given at a court case in Guildford in January 1597 (Old Style), equating to January 1598 in the modern calendar. The case concerned ownership of a certain plot of land and the court heard the testimony of a 59-year-old coroner, John Derrick, who gave witness that.

Being a scholler in the ffree schoole of Guldeford hee and diverse of his fellows did runne and play there at creckett and other plaies.

Given Derrick's age, it was about half a century earlier when he was at school and so it is certain that cricket was being played c. 1550 by boys in Surrey. The view that it was originally a children's game is reinforced by Randle Cotgrave's 1611 English-French dictionary in which he defined the noun "crosse" as "the crooked staff wherewith boys play at cricket" and the verb form "crosser" as "to play at cricket".

One possible source for the sport's name is the Old English word "cryce" (or "cricc") meaning a crutch or staff. In Samuel Johnson's Dictionary, he derived cricket from "cryce, Saxon, a stick". In Old French, the word "criquet" seems to have meant a kind of club or stick. Given the strong medieval trade connections between south-east England and the County of Flanders when the latter belonged to the Duchy of Burgundy, the name may have been derived from the Middle Dutch (in use in Flanders at the time) "krick"(-e), meaning a stick (crook). Another possible source is the Middle Dutch word "krickstoel", meaning a long low stool used for kneeling in church and which resembled the long low wicket with two stumps used in early cricket. According to Heiner Gillmeister, a European language expert of Bonn University, "cricket" derives from the Middle Dutch phrase for hockey, met de (krik ket)sen (i.e., "with the stick chase"). Gillmeister has suggested that not only the name but also the sport itself may be of Flemish origin.

- Growth of amateur and professional cricket in England

Evolution of the cricket bat. The original "hockey stick" (left) evolved into the straight bat from c. 1760 when pitched delivery bowling began.

Although the main object of the game has always been to score the most runs, the early form of cricket differed from the modern game in certain key technical aspects;

the North American variant of cricket known as wicket retained many of these aspects. The ball was bowled underarm by the bowler and along the ground towards a batter armed with a bat that in shape resembled a hockey stick; the batter defended a low, two-stump wicket; and runs were called notches because the scorers recorded them by notching tally sticks.

In 1611, the year Cotgrave's dictionary was published, ecclesiastical court records at Sidlesham in Sussex state that two parishioners, Bartholomew Wyatt and Richard Latter, failed to attend church on Easter Sunday because they were playing cricket. They were fined 12d each and ordered to do penance.This is the earliest mention of adult participation in cricket and it was around the same time that the earliest known organised inter-parish or village match was played – at Chevening, Kent. In 1624, a player called Jasper Vinall died after he was accidentally struck on the head during a match between two parish teams in Sussex.

Cricket remained a low-key local pursuit for much of the 17th century. It is known, through numerous references found in the records of ecclesiastical court cases, to have been proscribed at times by the Puritans before and during the Commonwealth. The problem was nearly always the issue of Sunday play as the Puritans considered cricket to be "profane" if played on the Sabbath, especially if large crowds or gambling were involved.

According to the social historian Derek Birley, there was a "great upsurge of sport after the Restoration" in 1660. Gambling on sport became a problem significant enough for Parliament to pass the 1664 Gambling Act, limiting stakes to £100 which was, in any case, a colossal sum exceeding the annual income of 99% of the population.

Along with prizefighting, horse racing and blood sports, cricket was perceived to be a gambling sport.Rich patrons made matches for high stakes, forming teams in which they engaged the first professional players.By the end of the century, cricket had developed into a major sport that was spreading throughout England and was already being taken abroad by English mariners and colonisers – the earliest reference to cricket overseas is dated 1676. A 1697 newspaper report survives of "a great cricket match" played in Sussex "for fifty guineas apiece" – this is the earliest known contest that is generally considered a First Class match.

- The patrons, and other players from the social class known as the "gentry", began to classify themselves as "amateurs" to establish a clear distinction from the professionals, who were invariably members of the working class, even to the point of having separate changing and dining facilities. The gentry, including such high-ranking nobles as the Dukes of Richmond, exerted their honour code of noblesse oblige to claim rights of leadership in any sporting contests they took part in, especially as it was necessary for them to play alongside their "social inferiors" if they were to win their bets. In time, a perception took hold that the typical amateur who played in first-class cricket, until 1962 when amateurism was abolished, was someone with a public school education who had then gone to one of Cambridge or Oxford University – society insisted that such people were "officers and gentlemen" whose destiny was to provide leadership. In a purely financial sense, the cricketing amateur would theoretically claim expenses for playing while his professional counterpart played under contract and was paid a wage or match fee; in practice, many amateurs claimed more than actual expenditure and the derisive term "shamateur" was coined to describe the practice.

• The Young Cricketer, 1768

The game underwent major development in the 18th century to become England's national sport.Its success was underwritten by the twin necessities of patronage and betting. Cricket was prominent in London as early as 1707 and, in the middle years of the century, large crowds flocked to matches on the Artillery Ground in Finsbury. The single wicket form of the sport attracted huge crowds and wagers to match, its popularity peaking in the 1748 season. Bowling underwent an evolution around 1760 when bowlers began to pitch the ball instead of rolling or skimming it towards the batter. This caused a revolution in bat design because, to deal with the bouncing ball, it was necessary to introduce the modern straight bat in place of the old "hockey stick" shape.

The Hambledon Club was founded in the 1760s and, for the next twenty years until the formation of Marylebone Cricket Club (MCC) and the opening of Lord's Old Ground in 1787, Hambledon was both the game's greatest club and its focal point. MCC quickly became the sport's premier club and the custodian of the Laws of Cricket. New Laws introduced in the latter part of the 18th century included the three stump wicket and leg before wicket (lbw).

The 19th century saw underarm bowling superseded by first roundarm and then overarm bowling. Both developments were controversial.Organisation of the game at county level led to the creation of the county clubs, starting with Sussex in 1839. In December 1889, the eight leading county clubs formed the official County Championship, which began in 1890.

The most famous player of the 19th century was W. G. Grace, who started his long and influential career in 1865. It was especially during the career of Grace that the distinction between amateurs and professionals became blurred by the existence of players like him who were nominally amateur but, in terms of their financial gain, de facto professional. Grace himself was said to have been paid more money for playing cricket than any professional.

The last two decades before the First World War have been called the "Golden Age of cricket". It is a nostalgic name prompted by the collective sense of loss resulting from the war, but the period did produce some great players and memorable matches, especially as organised competition at county and Test level developed.

- Cricket becomes an international sport

In 1844, the first-ever international match took place between the United States and Canada. In 1859, a team of English players went to North America on the first overseas tour. Meanwhile, the British Empire had been instrumental in spreading the game overseas and by the middle of the 19th century it had become well established in Australia, the Caribbean, India, Pakistan, New Zealand, North America and South Africa.

In 1862, an English team made the first tour of Australia. The first Australian team to travel overseas consisted of Aboriginal stockmen who toured England in 1868. The first One Day International match was played on 5 January 1971 between Australia and England at the Melbourne Cricket

Ground.

In 1876–77, an England team took part in what was retrospectively recognised as the first-ever Test match at the Melbourne Cricket Ground against Australia. The rivalry between England and Australia gave birth to The Ashes in 1882, and this has remained Test cricket's most famous contest. Test cricket began to expand in 1888–89 when South Africa played England.

- World cricket in the 20th century

The inter-war years were dominated by Australia's Don Bradman, statistically the greatest Test batter of all time. Test cricket continued to expand during the 20th century with the addition of the West Indies (1928), New Zealand (1930) and India (1932) before the Second World War and then Pakistan (1952), Sri Lanka (1982), Zimbabwe (1992), Bangladesh (2000), Ireland and Afghanistan (both 2018) in the post-war period. South Africa was banned from international cricket from 1970 to 1992 as part of the apartheid boycott.

- The rise of limited overs cricket

Cricket entered a new era in 1963 when English counties introduced the limited overs variant. As it was sure to produce a result, limited overs cricket was lucrative and the number of matches increased. The first Limited Overs International was played in 1971 and the governing International Cricket Council (ICC), seeing its potential, staged the first limited overs Cricket World Cup in 1975. In the 21st century, a new limited overs form, Twenty20, made an immediate impact. On 22 June 2017, Afghanistan and Ireland became the 11th and 12th ICC full members, enabling them to play Test cricket.

- A typical cricket field.

In cricket, the rules of the game are specified in a code called The Laws of Cricket (hereinafter called "the Laws") which has a global remit. There are 42 Laws (always written with a capital "L"). The earliest known version of the code was drafted in 1744 and, since 1788, it has been owned and maintained by its custodian, the Marylebone Cricket Club (MCC) in London.

- Playing area

Cricket is a bat-and-ball game played on a cricket field between two teams of eleven players each. The field is usually circular or oval in shape and the edge of the playing area is marked by a boundary, which may be a fence, part of the stands, a rope, a painted line or a combination of these; the boundary must if possible be marked along its entire length.

In the approximate centre of the field is a rectangular pitch (see image, below) on which a wooden target called a wicket is sited at each end; the wickets are placed 22 yards (20 m) apart. The pitch is a flat surface 10 feet (3.0 m) wide, with very short grass that tends to be worn away as the game progresses (cricket can also be played on artificial surfaces, notably matting). Each wicket is made of three wooden stumps topped by two bails.

- Cricket pitch and creases

As illustrated above, the pitch is marked at each end with four white painted lines: a bowling crease, a popping crease and two return creases. The three stumps are aligned centrally on the bowling crease, which is eight feet eight inches long. The popping crease is drawn four feet in front of the bowling crease and parallel to it; although it is drawn as a twelve-foot line (six feet either side of the wicket), it is, in fact, unlimited in length. The return creases are drawn at right angles to the popping crease so that they intersect the ends of the bowling crease; each return crease is drawn as an eight-foot line, so that it extends four feet behind the bowling crease, but is also, in fact, unlimited in length.

Before a match begins, the team captains (who are also players) toss a coin to decide which team will bat first and so take the first innings. Innings is the term used for each phase of play in the match.In each innings, one team bats, attempting to score runs, while the other team bowls and fields the ball, attempting to restrict the scoring and dismiss the batters. When the first innings ends, the teams change roles; there can be two to four innings depending upon the type of match. A match with four scheduled innings is played over three to five days; a match with two scheduled innings is usually completed in a single day. During an innings, all eleven members of the fielding team take the field, but usually only two members of the batting team are on the field at any given time. The exception to this is if a batter has any type of illness or injury restricting his or her ability to run, in this case the batter is allowed a runner who can run between the wickets when the batter hits a scoring run or runs,though this does not apply in international cricket. The order of batters is usually announced just before the match, but it can be varied.

The main objective of each team is to score more runs than their opponents but, in some forms of cricket, it is also necessary to dismiss all of the opposition batters in their final innings in order to win the match, which would otherwise be drawn. If the team batting last is all out having scored fewer runs than their opponents, they are said to have "lost by n runs" (where n is the difference between the aggregate number of runs scored by the teams). If the team that bats last scores enough runs to win, it is said to have "won by n wickets", where n is the number of wickets left to fall. For example, a team that passes its opponents' total having lost six wickets (i.e., six of their batters have been dismissed) have won the match "by four wickets".

In a two-innings-a-side match, one team's combined first and second innings total may be less than the other side's first innings total. The team with the greater score is then said to have "won by an innings and n runs", and does not need to bat again: n is the difference between the two teams' aggregate scores. If the team batting last is all out, and both sides have scored the same number of runs, then the match is a tie; this result is quite rare in matches of two innings a side with only 62 happening in first-class matches from the earliest known instance in 1741 until January 2017. In the traditional form of the game, if the time allotted for the match expires before either side can win, then the game is declared a draw.

If the match has only a single innings per side, then a maximum number of overs applies to each innings. Such a match is called a "limited overs" or "one-day" match, and the side scoring more runs wins regardless of the number of wickets lost, so that a draw cannot occur. In some cases, ties are broken by having each team bat for a one-over innings known as a Super Over; subsequent Super Overs may be played if the first Super Over ends in a tie. If this kind of match is temporarily interrupted by bad weather, then a complex mathematical formula, known as the Duckworth–Lewis–Stern method after its developers, is often used to recalculate a new target score. A one-day match can also be declared a "no-result" if fewer than a previously agreed number of overs have been bowled by either team, in circumstances that make normal resumption of play impossible; for example, wet weather.

In all forms of cricket, the umpires can abandon the match if bad light or rain makes it impossible to continue. There have been instances of entire matches, even Test matches scheduled to be played over five days, being lost to bad weather without a ball being bowled: for example, the third Test of the 1970/71 series in Australia.

- Innings

The innings (ending with 's' in both singular and plural form) is the term used for each phase of play during a match. Depending on the type of match being played, each team has either one or two innings. Sometimes all eleven members of the batting side take a turn to bat but, for various reasons, an innings can end before they have all done so. The innings terminates if the batting team is "all out", a term defined by the Laws: "at the fall of a wicket or the retirement of a batter, further balls remain to be bowled but no further batter is available to come in". In this situation, one of the batters has not been dismissed and is termed not out; this is because he has no partners left and there must always be two active batters while the innings is in progress.

- An innings may end early while there are still two not out batters

the batting team's captain may declare the innings closed even though some of his players have not had a turn to bat: this is a tactical decision by the captain, usually because he believes his team have scored sufficient runs and need time to dismiss the opposition in their innings

the set number of overs (i.e., in a limited overs match) have been bowled

the match has ended prematurely due to bad weather or running out of time

in the final innings of the match, the batting side has reached its target and won the game.

- Overs

The Laws state that, throughout an innings, "the ball shall be bowled from each end alternately in overs of 6 balls". The name "over" came about because the umpire calls "Over!" when six balls have been bowled. At this point, another bowler is deployed at the other end, and the fielding side changes ends while the batters do not. A bowler cannot bowl two successive overs, although a bowler can (and usually does) bowl alternate overs, from the same end, for several overs which are termed a "spell". The batters do not change ends at the end of the over, and so the one who was non-striker is now the striker and vice versa. The umpires also change positions so that the one who was at "square leg" now stands behind the wicket at the non-striker's end and vice versa.

- Clothing and equipment

English cricketer W. G. Grace "taking guard" in 1883. His pads and bat are very similar to those used today. The gloves have evolved somewhat. Many modern players use more defensive equipment than were available to Grace, most notably helmets and arm guards.

The wicket-keeper (a specialised fielder behind the batter) and the batters wear protective gear because of the hardness of the ball, which can be delivered at speeds of more than 145 kilometres per hour (90 mph) and presents a major health and safety concern. Protective clothing includes pads (designed to protect the knees and shins), batting gloves or wicket-keeper's gloves for the hands, a safety helmet for the head and a box for male players inside the trousers (to protect the crotch area). Some batters wear additional padding inside their shirts and trousers such as thigh pads, arm pads, rib protectors and shoulder pads. The only fielders allowed to wear protective gear are those in positions very close to the batter (i.e., if they are alongside or in front of him), but they cannot wear gloves or external leg guards.

Subject to certain variations, on-field clothing generally includes a collared shirt with short or long sleeves; long trousers; woolen pullover (if needed); cricket cap (for fielding) or a safety helmet; and spiked shoes or boots to increase traction. The kit is traditionally all white and this remains the case in Test and first-class cricket but, in limited overs cricket, team colours are worn instead.

- Bat and ball

Two types of cricket ball, both of the same size:

i) A used white ball. White balls are mainly used in limited overs cricket, especially in matches played at night, under floodlights (left).

ii) A used red ball. Red balls are used in Test cricket, first-class cricket and some other forms of cricket (right).

The essence of the sport is that a bowler delivers (i.e., bowls) the ball from his or her end of the pitch towards the batter who, armed with a bat, is "on strike" at the other end (see next sub-section: Basic gameplay).

The bat is made of wood, usually Salix alba (white willow), and has the shape of a blade topped by a cylindrical handle. The blade must not be more than 4.25 inches (10.8 cm) wide and the total length of the bat not more than 38 inches (97 cm). There is no standard for the weight, which is usually between 2 lb 7 oz and 3 lb (1.1 and 1.4 kg).

The ball is a hard leather-seamed spheroid, with a circumference of 9 inches (23 cm). The ball has a "seam": six rows of stitches attaching the leather shell of the ball to the string and cork interior. The seam on a new ball is prominent and helps the bowler propel it in a less predictable manner. During matches, the quality of the ball deteriorates to a point where it is no longer usable; during the course of this deterioration, its behaviour in flight will change and can influence the outcome of the match. Players will, therefore, attempt to modify the ball's behaviour by modifying its physical properties. Polishing the ball and wetting it with sweat or saliva is legal, even when the polishing is deliberately done on one side only to increase the ball's swing through the air, but the acts of rubbing other substances into the ball, scratching the surface or picking at the seam are illegal ball tampering.

- Player roles

Basic gameplay: bowler to batter

During normal play, thirteen players and two umpires are on the field. Two of the players are batters and the rest are all eleven members of the fielding team. The other nine players in the batting team are off the field in the pavilion. The image with overlay below shows what is happening when a ball is being bowled and which of the personnel are on or close to the pitch.

- Return crease

In the photo, the two batters (3 & 8; wearing yellow) have taken position at each end of the pitch (6). Three members of the fielding team (4, 10 & 11; wearing dark blue) are in shot. One of the two umpires (1; wearing white hat) is stationed behind the wicket (2) at the bowler's (4) end of the pitch. The bowler (4) is bowling the ball (5) from his end of the pitch to the batter at the other end who is called the "striker". The other batter (3) at the bowling end is called the "non-striker". The wicket-keeper (10), who is a specialist, is positioned behind the striker's wicket (9) and behind him stands one of the fielders in a position called "first slip" (11). While the bowler and the first slip are wearing conventional kit only, the two batters and the wicket-keeper are wearing protective gear including safety helmets, padded gloves and leg guards (pads).

While the umpire (1) in shot stands at the bowler's end of the pitch, his colleague stands in the outfield, usually in or near the fielding position called "square leg", so that he is in line with the popping crease (7) at the striker's end of the pitch. The bowling crease (not numbered) is the one on which the wicket is located between the return creases (12). The bowler (4) intends to hit the wicket (9) with the ball (5) or, at least, to prevent the striker (8) from scoring runs. The striker (8) intends, by using his bat, to defend his wicket and, if possible, to hit the ball away from the pitch in order to score runs.

Some players are skilled in both batting and bowling, or as either or these as well as wicket-keeping, so are termed all-rounders. Bowlers are classified according to their style, generally as fast bowlers, seam bowlers or spinners. Batters are classified according to whether they are right-handed or left-handed.

• Fielding

Of the eleven fielders, three are in shot in the image above. The other eight are elsewhere on the field, their positions determined on a tactical basis by the captain or the bowler. Fielders often change position between deliveries, again as directed by the captain or bowler.

If a fielder is injured or becomes ill during a match, a substitute is allowed to field instead of him, but the substitute cannot bowl or act as a captain, except in the case of concussion substitutes in international cricket. The substitute leaves the field when the injured player is fit to return. The Laws of Cricket were updated in 2017 to allow substitutes to act as wicket-keepers.

• Bowling and dismissal

Glenn McGrath of Australia holds the world record for most wickets in the Cricket World Cup.

Most bowlers are considered specialists in that they are selected for the team because of their skill as a bowler, although some are all-rounders and even specialist batters bowl occasionally. The specialists bowl several times during an innings but may not bowl two overs consecutively. If the captain wants a bowler to "change ends", another bowler must temporarily fill in so that the change is not immediate.

A bowler reaches his delivery stride by means of a "run-up" and an over is deemed to have begun when the bowler starts his run-up for the first delivery of that over, the ball then being "in play".

Fast bowlers, needing momentum, take a lengthy run up while bowlers with a slow delivery take no more than a couple of steps before bowling. The fastest bowlers can deliver the ball at a speed of over 145 kilometres per hour (90 mph) and they sometimes rely on sheer speed to try to defeat the batter, who is forced to react very quickly.

Other fast bowlers rely on a mixture of speed and guile by making the ball seam or swing (i.e. curve) in flight. This type of delivery can deceive a batter into miscuing his shot, for example, so that the ball just touches the edge of the bat and can then be "caught behind" by the wicket-keeper or a slip fielder. At the other end of the bowling scale is the spin bowler who bowls at a relatively slow pace and relies entirely on guile to deceive the batter. A spinner will often "buy his wicket" by "tossing one up" (in a slower, steeper parabolic path) to lure the batter into making a poor shot. The batter has to be very wary of such deliveries as they are often "flighted" or spun so that the ball will not behave quite as he expects and he could be "trapped" into getting himself out. In between the pacemen and the spinners are the medium paced seamers who rely on persistent accuracy to try to contain the rate of scoring and wear down the batter's concentration.

There are nine ways in which a batter can be dismissed: five relatively common and four extremely rare. The common forms of dismissal are bowled, caught, leg before wicket (lbw), run out and stumped. Rare methods are hit wicket,hit the ball twice, obstructing the field and timed out. The Laws state that the fielding team, usually the bowler in practice, must appeal for a dismissal before the umpire can give his decision. If the batter is out, the umpire raises a forefinger and says "Out!"; otherwise, he will shake his head and say "Not out".There is, effectively, a tenth method of dismissal, retired out, which is not an on-field dismissal as such but rather a retrospective one for which no fielder is credited.

- Batting, runs and extras

The directions in which a right-handed batter, facing down the page, intends to send the ball when playing various cricketing shots. The diagram for a left-handed batter is a mirror image of this one.

Batters take turns to bat via a batting order which is decided beforehand by the team captain and presented to the umpires, though the order remains flexible when the captain officially nominates the team. Substitute batters are generally not allowed, except in the case of concussion substitutes in international cricket.

In order to begin batting the batter first adopts a batting stance. Standardly, this involves adopting a slight crouch with the feet pointing across the front of the wicket, looking in the direction of the bowler, and holding the bat so it passes over the feet and so its tip can rest on the ground near to the toes of the back foot.

A skilled batter can use a wide array of "shots" or "strokes" in both defensive and attacking mode. The idea is to hit the ball to the best effect with the flat surface of the bat's blade. If the ball touches the side of the bat it is called an "edge". The batter does not have to play a shot and can allow the ball to go through to the wicketkeeper. Equally, he does not have to attempt a run when he hits the ball with his bat. Batters do not always seek to hit the ball as hard as possible, and a good player can score runs just by making a deft stroke with a turn of the wrists or by simply "blocking" the ball but directing it away from fielders so that he has time to take a run. A wide variety of shots are played, the batter's repertoire including strokes named according to the style of swing and the direction aimed: e.g., "cut", "drive", "hook", "pull".

The batter on strike (i.e. the "striker") must prevent the ball hitting the wicket, and try to score runs by hitting the ball with his bat so that he and his partner have time to run from one end of the pitch to the other before the fielding side can return the ball. To register a run, both runners must touch the ground behind the popping crease with either their bats or their bodies (the batters carry their bats as they run). Each completed run increments the score of both the team and the striker.

- Sachin Tendulkar is the only player to have scored one hundred international centuries

The decision to attempt a run is ideally made by the batter who has the better view of the ball's progress, and this is communicated by calling: usually "yes", "no" or "wait". More than one run can be scored from a single hit: hits worth one to three runs are common, but the size of the field is such that it is usually difficult to run four or more. To compensate for this, hits that reach the boundary of the field are automatically awarded four runs if the ball touches the ground en route to the boundary or six runs if the ball clears the boundary without touching the ground within the boundary. In these cases the batters do not need to run. Hits for five are unusual and generally rely on the help of "overthrows" by a fielder returning the ball. If an odd number of runs is scored by the striker, the two batters have changed ends, and the one who was non-striker is now the striker. Only the striker can score individual runs, but all runs are added to the team's total.

Additional runs can be gained by the batting team as extras (called "sundries" in Australia) due to errors made by the fielding side. This is achieved in four ways: no-ball, a penalty of one extra conceded by the bowler if he breaks the rules; wide, a penalty of one extra conceded by the bowler if he bowls so that the ball is out of the batter's reach bye, an extra awarded if the batter misses the ball and it goes past the wicket-keeper and gives the batters time to run in the conventional way leg bye, as for a bye except that the ball has hit the batter's body, though not his bat. If the bowler has conceded a no-ball or a wide, his team incurs an additional penalty because that ball (i.e., delivery) has to be bowled again and hence the batting side has the opportunity to score more runs from this extra ball.

- Specialist roles

Captain (cricket) and Wicket-keeper
The captain is often the most experienced player in the team, certainly the most tactically astute, and can possess any of the main skillsets as a batter, a bowler or a wicket-

keeper. Within the Laws, the captain has certain responsibilities in terms of nominating his players to the umpires before the match and ensuring that his players conduct themselves "within the spirit and traditions of the game as well as within the Laws".

The wicket-keeper (sometimes called simply the "keeper") is a specialist fielder subject to various rules within the Laws about his equipment and demeanour. He is the only member of the fielding side who can effect a stumping and is the only one permitted to wear gloves and external leg guards. Depending on their primary skills, the other ten players in the team tend to be classified as specialist batters or specialist bowlers. Generally, a team will include five or six specialist batters and four or five specialist bowlers, plus the wicket-keeper.

- Umpires and scorers

The game on the field is regulated by the two umpires, one of whom stands behind the wicket at the bowler's end, the other in a position called "square leg" which is about 15–20 metres away from the batter on strike and in line with the popping crease on which he is taking guard. The umpires have several responsibilities including adjudication on whether a ball has been correctly bowled (i.e., not a no-ball or a wide); when a run is scored; whether a batter is out (the fielding side must first appeal to the umpire, usually with the phrase "How's that?" or "Owzat?"); when intervals start and end; and the suitability of the pitch, field and weather for playing the game. The umpires are authorised to interrupt or even abandon a match due to circumstances likely to endanger the players, such as a damp pitch or deterioration of the light.

Off the field in televised matches, there is usually a third umpire who can make decisions on certain incidents with the aid of video evidence. The third umpire is mandatory under the playing conditions for Test and Limited Overs International matches played between two ICC full member countries. These matches also have a match referee whose job is to ensure that play is within the Laws and the spirit of the game.

The match details, including runs and dismissals, are recorded by two official scorers, one representing each team. The scorers are directed by the hand signals of an umpire . For example, the umpire raises a forefinger to signal that the batter is out (has been dismissed); he raises both arms above his head if the batter has hit the ball for six runs. The scorers are required by the Laws to record all runs scored, wickets taken and overs bowled; in practice, they also note significant amounts of additional data relating to the game.

A match's statistics are summarised on a scorecard. Prior to the popularisation of scorecards, most scoring was done by men sitting on vantage points cuttings notches on tally sticks and runs were originally called notches.According to Rowland Bowen, the earliest known scorecard templates were introduced in 1776 by T. Pratt of Sevenoaks and soon came into gencral use.It is believed that scorecards were printed and sold at Lord's for the first time in 1846.

- thank you for buy & read this book

  have a great day of your
  from : Mr Vivek Kumar Pandey

- This All Credit Goes To My Super Hero Daddy. "Always Love You dad'.

www.ingramcontent.com/pod-product-compliance
Lightning Source LLC
Chambersburg PA
CBHW022122150726
47990CB00003B/1460